Grayslake Area Public Library District
Grayslake, Illinois

1. A fine will be charged on each book which is not returned when it is due.

2. All injuries to books beyond reasonable wear and all losses shall be made good to the satisfaction of the Librarian.

3. Each borrower is held responsible for all books drawn on his card and for all fines accruing on the same.

Dear Parent:

Congratulations! Your child is taking the first steps on an exciting journey. The destination? Independent reading!

STEP INTO READING® will help your child get there. The program offers five steps to reading success. Each step includes fun stories and colorful art. There are also Step into Reading Sticker Books, Step into Reading Math Readers, Step into Reading Write-In Readers, Step into Reading Phonics Readers, and Step into Reading Phonics First Steps! Boxed Sets—a complete literacy program with something for every child.

Learning to Read, Step by Step!

Ready to Read Preschool–Kindergarten
• big type and easy words • rhyme and rhythm • picture clues
For children who know the alphabet and are eager to begin reading.

Reading with Help Preschool–Grade 1
• basic vocabulary • short sentences • simple stories
For children who recognize familiar words and sound out new words with help.

Reading on Your Own Grades 1–3
• engaging characters • easy-to-follow plots • popular topics
For children who are ready to read on their own.

Reading Paragraphs Grades 2–3
• challenging vocabulary • short paragraphs • exciting stories
For newly independent readers who read simple sentences with confidence.

Ready for Chapters Grades 2–4
• chapters • longer paragraphs • full-color art
For children who want to take the plunge into chapter books but still like colorful pictures.

STEP INTO READING® is designed to give every child a successful reading experience. The grade levels are only guides. Children can progress through the steps at their own speed, developing confidence in their reading, no matter what their grade.

Remember, a lifetime love of reading starts with a single step!

For Mom and Dad "A"
—M.L.

www.stepintoreading.com
www.randomhouse.com/kids/disney

Educators and librarians, for a variety of teaching tools, visit us at
www.randomhouse.com/teachers

Library of Congress Cataloging-in-Publication Data
Lagonegro, Melissa.
Sealed with a kiss / by Melissa Lagonegro; illustrated by Elisa Marrucchi.
    p. cm. — (Step into reading. A step 2 book)
ISBN: 0-7364-2363-X (pbk.) ISBN: 0-7364-8047-1 (lib. bdg.)
[1. Mermaids—Juvenile fiction.] I. Marrucchi, Elisa. II. Title. III. Series: Step into reading. Step 2 book.
PZ7.L14317Sea 2005 2005001947

Printed in the United States of America   20 19 18 17

STEP INTO READING, RANDOM HOUSE, and the Random House colophon are registered trademarks of Random House, Inc.

DISNEY
✦ PRINCESS

Sealed with a Kiss

by Melissa Lagonegro
illustrated by Elisa Marrucchi

Random House 🏠 New York

Ariel and Flounder
love to play
hide-and-seek
under the sea.

They want the baby seal
to play with them.
Ariel points
to where the seal
could be.

The two friends
swim to find him.

They find the seal!
He is sitting
on a rock.
He cannot wait
to play hide-and-seek.

"One, two, three . . . ,"
Ariel starts to count.
The others hide.

"Ready or not,
here I come,"
she says.

Ariel looks
in the seaweed.
She searches
in the sea plants.

"Gotcha!"
cries Ariel.
She has found
Flounder!

Now Ariel
has to find
the baby seal.

Where can he be?

She looks
inside a chest.
She sees many things.
But no baby seal.

Ariel looks
under a rock cliff.
She sees
a sleeping blowfish.
But no baby seal.

Ariel hears music.
She sees fish
dancing and singing.
But no baby seal!

Ariel even goes

back to the rock.

She sees Scuttle.

But <u>no</u> baby seal!

Squeak! Squeak!

"What is that noise?"

asks Ariel.

They swim
to find out.

Oh, no!

It is the baby seal.

He is stuck!

His tail is caught

in a giant clamshell.

Ariel tries
to open the shell.
She lifts!
She pulls!

She does it!
Ariel sets
the seal free!

Ariel is happy
she has found
the seal.
And the seal
is <u>very</u> happy
to be found.

Ariel gives
her friend
a big hug.

She seals it with a kiss!